FEB '94

CH

OCTOPUS HUG

by *Laurence Pringle*

Boyds Mills Press

Illustrated by *Kate Salley Palmer*

Published by Caroline House

Boyds Mills Press, Inc.

A Highlights Company

910 Church Street

Honesdale, Pennsylvania 18431

Printed in Mexico

Publisher Cataloging-in-Publication Data

Pringle, Laurence.

Octopus hug / by Laurence Pringle ;

illustrated by Kate Salley Palmer.—1st ed.

[32]p. : col. ill. ; cm.

Summary: When Mom goes out for the evening,

Dad and the kids invent games

filled with fun and laughter, and they all

learn how to give an octopus hug.

ISBN 1-56397-034-1

1. Family life—Juvenile fiction.

2. Fathers—Juvenile fiction.

[1. Family life. 2. Fathers.] I. Palmer, Kate Salley, ill.

II. Title.

[E]—dc20   1993

Library of Congress Catalog Card Number: 92-73830

First edition, 1993

Book designed by Joy Chu

The text of this book is set in 16-point Century Old Style.

The display type is set in Casablanca Light Condensed with Simoncini Garamond Italics.

The illustrations are done in colored pencil.

Distributed by St. Martin's Press

10 9 8 7 6 5 4 3 2 1

To Heidi, Jeffrey, Sean, Jesse, and Rebecca—
with fond memories of Cloud, Prison Break, and
all the other games we played —L.P.

To James and Salley—K.S.P.

"Good-bye, Jesse.
    Good-bye, Becky."
My mother was going out to have dinner with a friend.
Dad was taking care of my sister and me.
Mom kissed us all good-bye.

After she left, I felt sad and grumpy.
Becky and I began to fight.
Dad asked, "How many arms does an octopus have?"

"Eight," I said.

"Well," he said, "you are about to be hugged by an octopus!"

He wrapped two arms around my middle.
"One, two," he counted.
Then he moved one arm and
wrapped it around my legs.
"Three." He wrapped
the other around my
head. "Four."

Dad's arms kept moving and hugging. "Five . . . six . . . seven . . . eight." Finally the octopus gave me a big squeeze and let me go.

Then we sat on Dad's lap in the rocking chair,
and he started to sing a lullaby.
Becky did not feel like singing.

Instead of singing "Rock-a-bye, Baby,"
Dad sang "Rock-a-bye,
Sweetie Pies."

When he sang the part
about the bough breaking
and the cradle and the
sweetie pies coming down,
we had a big surprise.

We all fell out of the chair
onto the rug!

"There's something wrong
with this chair," said Dad.
"Let's try it again."

This time we all sang.
At the end of the
song the chair tossed
us out again!

Dad tried another song that he called
"She'll Be Falling down the Mountain
When She Comes." As we stopped singing,
sure enough, we all fell onto the floor.

Dad figured out why this happened. Whenever
we sang a song about falling, he explained,
the chair made us fall onto the rug. We rocked,
sang, and fell on the floor many times. Then
we all lay on the rug and rested.

But not for long. Our strange
rocking chair had reminded me of
another game we play with Dad.
"Let's play tree," I said.

Dad knelt on the rug and held his hands at his sides, palms up, like low tree limbs. I put a foot on each limb, and he lifted the limbs high enough for me to climb up on his shoulders—to the top of the tree.

Then Dad made a whistling sound like the wind. The tree started to sway, first to one side then the other. The wind blew harder, and the tree swayed farther. I hung on tight! Crack! The old tree began to fall. Dad yelled, "Timber!"
The tree fell toward the couch, and I landed on soft cushions.

Soon the tree stood again, with its low limbs
ready for another climber.

"Be a monster," said Becky
when she grew tired of
the tree game.

Dad growled. "Now I have you," he said as he held Becky's shoulders
down on the rug. But he left her feet free to reach his chest. She
pushed with all her might and sent the monster tumbling backward.

He caught us again and again. We were strong enough to escape
from the monster every time.

As Dad lay flat on his back, I thought of another game.
I yelled, "Put a quarter in!"

Becky and I scrambled onto Dad's stomach and chest. He pretended he was a riding machine like the ones at the supermarket. He opened his mouth and I pretended to put in a quarter to start the machine.

The riding machine rose and began to sway and bounce. It moved from side to side and up and down. Soon it tipped us off on the rug. It kept moving, and we tried to get back on. Just as I clambered aboard, it shut down. I let Becky get on, too, then we put in a second quarter.

Another wild ride began! After several rides the machine broke
down. It would not move. I think this happens because Dad gets tired.

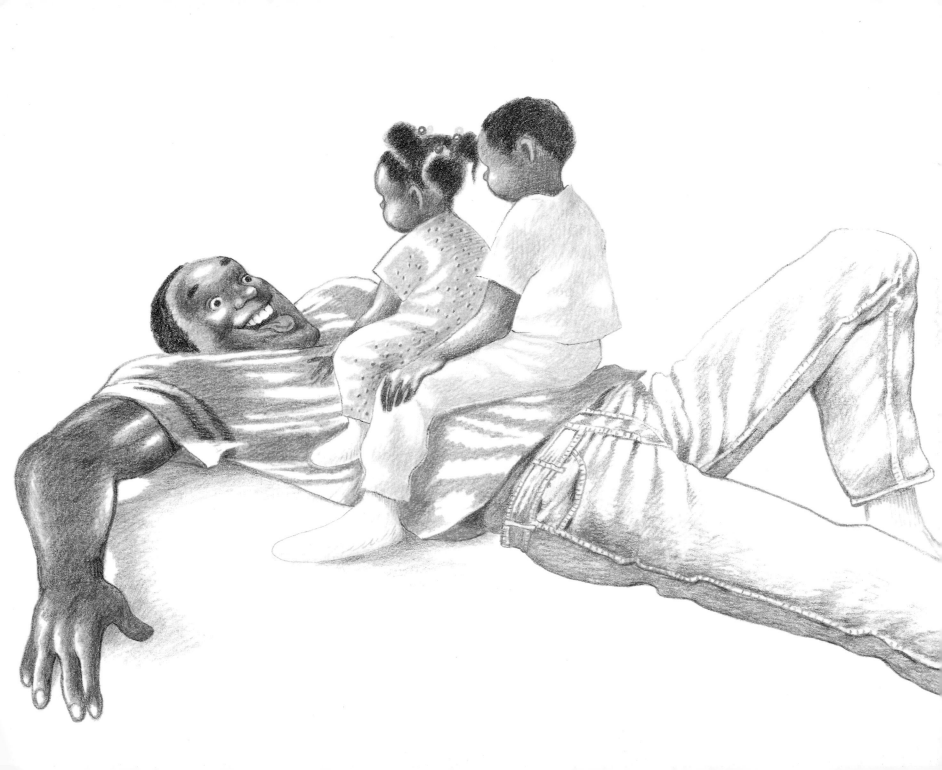

Dad went to get a drink of water. When he returned, he pretended
to stumble over Becky on the rug. "Those kids," he said.
"They always leave their toys around the house!
I almost fell over one of Becky's
stuffed animals!"

He picked up Becky and dropped her among
the real stuffed animals on her bed.
I hurried to lie down in his path so
he could pretend to trip over me.

"Another one!" Dad said.
He picked me up, slung
me over his shoulder, and
tossed me onto my bed.
Becky and I raced to sprawl
on the floor again and again.
Dad kept tripping over us.
He complained about the dolls
and stuffed animals on the floor
and carried us back to
our beds again and again.

"Now," said Dad, "it is *really* time for bed." He promised us one more game once we were ready to settle down for the night.

When Dad came to my bed, I asked for "animal bridge." I lay on my stomach under the covers. "A mouse," I said, and Dad's fingers scampered over my body, from my feet to my head.

"A frog." His hand hopped, hopped, hopped over the animal bridge. I asked for other animals: a cat, a snake, even an elephant!

Then Mom returned. She came in to say good night. Becky was already asleep. "How did it go?" she asked. "Did you have a good time with Daddy?"

"Yes," I said. "We played animal bridge and pretended to be toys left on the floor that Dad had to pick up, and we played put-a-quarter-in, and monster, and tree, and 'Rock-a-bye, Sweetie Pies,' and octopus hug!"

Mom laughed. "What on earth is an octopus hug?" she asked.

So Dad gave her one.